# Snowstar and the Big Freeze

# To Sophie Simpson

·★·★·

# Special thanks to Conrad Mason

ORCHARD BOOKS

First published in Great Britain in 2019 by The Watts Publishing Group

1 3 5 7 9 10 8 6 4 2

Text copyright © 2019 Working Partners Limited
Illustrations © Orchard Books 2019
Series created by Working Partners Limited

A CIP catalogue record for this book is available from the British Library.

ISBN 978 1 40835 708 8

Printed and bound in Great Britain by Clays Ltd, Elcograf S.p.A.

Orchard Books
An imprint of Hachette Children's Group
Part of The Watts Publishing Group Limited
Carmelite House
50 Victoria Embankment
London EC4Y 0DZ

An Hachette UK Company
www.hachette.co.uk
www.hachettechildrens.co.uk

# Snowstar and
# the Big Freeze

## Daisy Meadows

ORCHARD

Contents

Story One:
# Winter Presents

## Story Two:
# Winter Snow

## Story Three:
# Winter Feast

# Meet the Characters

Aisha and Emily are best friends from Spellford Village. Aisha loves sports, whilst Emily's favourite thing is science. But what both girls enjoy more than anything is visiting Enchanted Valley and helping their unicorn friends who live there.

Snowstar

Snowstar is a white foal with big blue eyes. His golden horn isn't fully grown yet. He is too young to have magic of his own or fly, so he's very impatient to grow up!

Wintertail the Winter Unicorn has three lockets which control presents, snow and feasts. Winter is her favourite time of year – she never gets cold.

Wintertail

Queen Aurora is the queen of Enchanted Valley and in charge of friendship; there's nothing more important than her friends. She has a silver crown, and a beautiful coat which can change colour.

Queen Aurora

Selena is a wicked unicorn who will do anything to become queen of Enchanted Valley. She'll even steal the magical lockets if she has to. She won't give them back until the unicorns crown her queen.

Selena

Spellford

Enchanted Valley

Enchanted Cottage

Golden Palace

An Enchanted Valley lies a twinkle away,
Where beautiful unicorns live, laugh and play
You can visit the mermaids, or go for a ride,
So much fun to be had, but dangers can hide!

Your friends need your help – this is how you know:
A keyring lights up with a magical glow.
Whirled off like a dream, you won't want to leave.
Friendship forever, when you truly believe.

## STORY ONE

## WINTER PRESENTS

# Chapter One
# Snow

Aisha Khan and her best friend, Emily Turner, stood in Aisha's garden, staring up at the grey sky.

"Come on, snow!" they wished together.

The air was freezing cold, and their breath puffed like dragon smoke. They shivered a little even though they were

wearing coats. The grassy lawn behind
Aisha's house, Enchanted Cottage, was
white with frost, but the air was clear. "It's
so cold, I wonder why there's no snow?"
she said.

"Perhaps the air is too dry," said Emily.
"It needs to be damp for the ice crystals
to form and make snowflakes."

Aisha smiled. "Did you read that in one

of your science books?"

"How did you guess?" laughed Emily.
She loved science, almost as much as
Aisha loved playing sport.

Aisha lowered her voice. "Do you think
they have winter in Enchanted Valley?"
she whispered.

"Oh, I bet it looks beautiful all covered
in snow!" said Emily.

The girls grinned at each other.
Enchanted Valley was a magical world
full of unicorns and other fantastical
creatures. And best of all, no one knew
about it but them.

"I hope we'll be able to visit again
soon," said Aisha. She dug in her pocket
and pulled out the magical keyring that

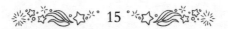

transported her to Enchanted Valley. Emily brought hers out too. From each keyring dangled two charms – one shaped like a unicorn, and the other like a crystal. They glittered like ice in the light.

"I don't know which is prettier," whispered Emily.

The two unicorn keyrings had been given to them by Queen Aurora herself, and the two crystal charms were gifts from the Nature Unicorns, to thank the girls for getting their magical lockets back. The wicked unicorn Selena had stolen them as part of her plan to become

Queen of Enchanted Valley.

"Oh!" gasped Aisha suddenly.

The little unicorn on each keyring had begun to glow with a strange, fiery light.

Emily's heart raced. "Queen Aurora needs us!" she said.

They ran behind the stone statue of a phoenix in the middle of the garden, and checked their keyrings. Both unicorns were glowing brighter than ever now.

"Ready?" asked Emily.

"Ready!" said Aisha.

The girls touched the two unicorn horns together.

*Whhhhhhhssshhh!*

There was a sudden flash of golden
light, and sparkles exploded all around
them like fireworks. The girls laughed as
they felt themselves lifting off the ground.

A moment later, their feet came down
with a soft crunch on pure white snow.

"Look!" cried Emily excitedly.

There was snow everywhere, as far as
they could see. It lay like a thick layer
of icing on the ground and fell in soft
flurries through the crisp, cold air.

The girls stood on a slope, looking up at the beautiful Golden Palace, where Queen Aurora lived. Its towers were dusted with a light sprinkling of snow, and even the flowers that grew against the walls glittered with frost.

"You were right," said Aisha. "It does look beautiful!"

The girls scrambled up the hill, their feet sinking deep into the snow. As they reached the castle, the drawbridge swung down over the frozen moat, and Queen Aurora stepped out on to it.

Emily gasped. Queen Aurora's coat was even more beautiful in winter — it shifted from deep red to gold, bright yellow and pink, like the cosy fire in Enchanted

Cottage. Her golden horn gleamed, and her silver crown sparkled in the icy light.

"Welcome, girls!" she said. She dipped her head in greeting, and her magical locket, with two tiny golden suns in it, caught the light. The girls knew it gave Aurora the power to protect friendship throughout Enchanted Valley.

"Hello, Queen Aurora! Is everything all right?" Aisha asked anxiously.

"I hope Selena isn't causing trouble again," added Emily.

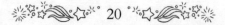

Queen Aurora smiled and shook her head, making her golden mane shimmer. "She's nowhere to be seen, thanks to you girls. Actually, I invited you here to have some fun! Follow me …"

As Queen Aurora trotted along the banks of the ice-covered moat, the girls exchanged a glance then followed, wondering what she meant.

When they reached the back of the castle, Aisha gasped in astonishment. "Wow!"

On the hillside, a party was in full swing. The girls didn't know what to look at first! Icy blue fairy lights dangled between the trees all around the snowy slope, where the unicorns mingled –

prancing, tossing their manes and playing games. It looked like so much fun!

There were giant ice sculptures of dragons with heaps of presents piled beneath them. There were sledging competitions, and ice rinks. Little stalls sold brightly coloured snow cones, and blue banners decorated with snowflakes fluttered in the wind. Delicious smells hung in the air: hot chocolate mixed up

with popcorn and roasting chestnuts.

"It's the most amazing party I've ever seen!" cried Emily.

"And you're both invited!" said Queen Aurora. She led them through the snow to the entrance. Holly bushes grew on each side, shaped like unicorns and sprinkled with snow.

As they stood there, marvelling at the party, a pure white unicorn trotted over.

A tiny white unicorn with big blue eyes cantered behind her. His mane was short and fluffy, and his horn was only a little golden nub.

"It's a foal!" whispered Aisha.

"A unicorn foal!" added Emily.

"He's so cute!" they said together.

"This is Wintertail, the Winter Unicorn," said Aurora, as the big white unicorn approached. "And this is her foal, Snowstar. They're hosting the party!"

Wintertail dipped her head and glittering silver horn in greeting. Her coat shone, even against the snow. "I've heard so much about you two," said Wintertail. "You're heroes!"

Little Snowstar reared up eagerly.

"Hello there!" he whinnied. "And welcome to the Winter Festival!"

# Chapter Two
# Three Lockets

"Winter Festival?" said Emily, grinning. "That sounds amazing."

"It is amazing!" said Snowstar proudly. "We have it every year, when my mum's magic brings a perfect winter to Enchanted Valley."

The girls saw that Wintertail had a

chain around her neck, just like every other unicorn. But instead of one magical locket hanging from the chain—

"You have three lockets!" gasped Aisha.

"That's right," said Wintertail, smiling. "Take a look, if you'd like."

Aisha gently lifted the closest locket. It had a tiny present inside, gift-wrapped in sparkly green paper, with a silver bow.

"That's the Winter Presents locket," said Snowstar. "It's my favourite! The Winter Snow locket and the Winter Feast lockets are my favourite too!"

The girls laughed. Emily peered closer. The Winter Feast locket had a shiny red-and-white candy cane inside, and in the Snow locket was a tiny snowflake. It

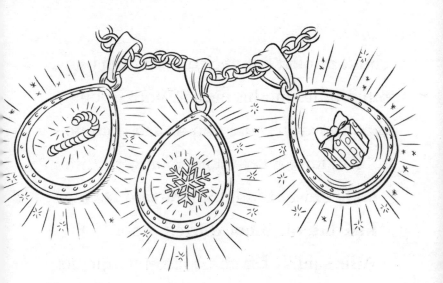

was gently spinning, just like the paper snowflakes they had made at school recently. "They're beautiful," said Emily.

"Thank you!" said Wintertail, flicking her tail happily. "The Winter Presents locket makes sure everyone gets the right gift. The Winter Snow locket brings just enough snow to have fun in, and the Winter Feast locket makes plenty of yummy winter treats for everyone!"

Aisha noticed that Snowstar didn't have a chain around his neck. "What about you, Snowstar?" she asked. "Do you use your magic to help your mum?"

Snowstar's head hung low, and he scraped at the snow with his hoof. "Oh no," he said. "I haven't got my magic yet. I can't even fly. Unless …" He trotted in a circle and leapt up high … but he just landed back in the snow with a flumph. "Oh, candy canes!" he said. "I thought it might work that time."

"I'm sure it won't be long

now, little one," said Wintertail, nuzzling Snowstar with her soft white nose.

"We unicorns aren't born with our magic," Queen Aurora explained. "We get it as we grow up."

"And when I do, I'll find out what my special talent is!" said Snowstar. He swished his tail, looking cheerful again. "I can't wait."

"You're still helpful, even without magic," said Wintertail. "This year, Snowstar hung up all the twinkly lights."

"They're beautiful," Aisha told him.

Suddenly a fierce wind whipped through the Festival, shaking the fairy lights and jingling the sleigh bells. Emily and Aisha shivered in the now biting

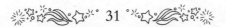

cold. The unicorns huddled together in groups, their tails and manes blowing in all directions.

"What was that?" wondered Aisha.

Then something flashed down from the sky, like a bolt of lightning. *Thump!* A silver unicorn landed nearby, her hooves kicking up a spray of snow. Her mane and tail were deep blue, and her purple eyes gleamed.

The girls' hearts sank.

"Selena!" whispered Emily. "What's she doing here?"

Selena trotted in a circle. Her coat shimmered and crackled with electricity, and the girls caught sight of her locket, flashing with the tiny lightning bolts

contained inside.

"I don't like this," whimpered Snowstar, his ears flattened against his head as he ducked behind the girls.

"Unicorns of Enchanted Valley!" boomed Selena. "Tremble before your true Queen! I have come to—"

"—eat all your food!" squeaked a tiny

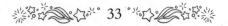

voice.

A little white creature hopped down from Selena's back. It had a long snout, small dark eyes and fluffy fur. Its tail waved as it scampered over to a big pile of roasted chestnuts and began to gobble them up.

"That's an arctic fox," said Emily. "I've never seen one in real life before!"

"I'm not here for the food, stupid

animal," Selena growled at the fox. The
fox skulked back to her. "I've come to
ruin your precious Winter Festival," she
roared at the unicorns. "Now winter will
be miserable for ever … unless you make
me Queen of Enchanted Valley!"

Before the girls could do anything,
Selena lowered her head. *Fffffzzzapp!*
A bolt of white lightning shot straight
from her horn and hit the chain around
Wintertail's neck. *Whhooooosh!* The three
lockets shot through the air like comets,
trailing icy sparks. A moment later they
had disappeared beyond the horizon.

"Where have they gone?" gasped Aisha.

"You'll never find out!" crowed Selena.
"They're hidden now, all around the

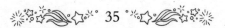

Valley. Not even you meddling girls will be able to find them!"

"Urgh!"

The girls turned to see a yellow unicorn spit out a candy cane. "It tastes yucky now," said the unicorn.

"Oh no!"

Nearby, a pale green unicorn had just finished unwrapping a present. Inside was

 a dirty metal bucket with a large hole in the bottom. "It was a beautiful hairbrush just a second ago," the unicorn explained.

"Then it turned into this!"

"Now Selena has my lockets, the magic is doing the opposite of what it's supposed to," said Wintertail in despair. "All the delicious food is turning horrible! The presents are becoming awful! And ..."

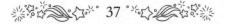

Before she could finish, the wind began to howl across the hillside. It rustled the branches of the trees, knocked over food stalls and made the unicorns shiver with cold. The snow fell harder and harder, and the delicate snowflakes turned into large chunks of snow and ice.

"It's a blizzard!" wailed Queen Aurora.

"Say goodbye to your Winter Festival!" laughed Selena. "Oh, and just to make sure you can't stop me … say goodbye to Wintertail, too!"

The wicked unicorn lowered her horn a second time.

*Ffffzzzzaaap!* Another blast of lightning shot out and struck Wintertail. There was a flash of bright white light all around,

and the girls blinked.

When they looked again, they both gasped. The snow-white unicorn had vanished!

# Chapter Three
# Socks for a Mermaid

"What have you done with Wintertail?" cried Emily, over the roar of the blizzard.

"She's now locked in my castle," sneered Selena, "where you'll never be able to rescue her! Come on, Blizz," she called to the arctic fox, "we've got our own little Winter Festival to plan." She reared up, cackling with laughter. Another bolt of lightning shot from her horn and struck the fairy lights. *Bang!* They all blinked out.

Blizz raced across the snow and hopped on to his mistress's back, still chewing chestnuts. Then Selena launched herself up into the air. With a fizz and a crackle of electricity, she was gone.

In the silence that followed, the girls heard quiet, sniffling sounds.

Aisha turned and saw Snowstar still cowering behind her. The poor little foal hung his head, his eyes glistening with tears. "I want my mum back," he said sadly.

Emily threw her arms around the foal's warm neck and hugged him tight.

"Don't worry," she
whispered. "We'll
save her."

"And we'll save
the Winter Festival,
too," added Aisha.
"We'll get those
lockets back!"

"Oh, thank you, girls," said Queen
Aurora. "You're so brave! But you'll need
some warmer clothes in this terrible
cold." She lowered her head, and a warm
golden light shone at the tip of her horn,
encircling the girls in sparkles.

They looked down at themselves in
surprise. Their coats and trousers had
transformed into thick, cosy snowsuits.

"This is much better," said Aisha happily. "I can feel my toes again!"

"We should hurry, before the snow gets worse," said Emily.

Sure enough, the snow was falling thicker and faster now.

"Wait for me!" said Snowstar. The girls turned to see the little foal trot over, his head raised bravely. "I know I'm little, but I have to help rescue my mum!"

"In that case …" said Queen Aurora. She waved her horn a second time, and a golden scarf appeared around Snowstar's neck in a flurry of magical sparkles.

"Selena's castle lies to the west, beyond the mountain range," said Aurora. "That's where you'll find Wintertail. Good luck, all of you!"

The other unicorns joined in with a
chorus of good wishes.

"Thank you, girls!"

"Have courage, Snowstar!"

"Don't give up hope!"

The girls weren't going to give up until
they'd saved Wintertail, and saved winter
too.

⋆ ⋆

The blizzard swirled around them as the girls and Snowstar headed west. They peered into it with narrowed eyes, but they couldn't see anything but whiteness. It was getting harder and harder to wade through it.

"It's almost up to my waist!" said Emily, panting.

"If only I could fly us there," said Snowstar sadly.

"It wouldn't matter," said Aisha. "Even a grown-up unicorn would struggle flying in this horrible weather. We're better off walking."

Snowstar looked relieved at this.

"What's that?" said Emily suddenly. She pointed at something shiny and red,

sticking out of the snow.

"There's another one!" said Aisha. "But it's green."

The girls fought through the snow. When they reached the little objects, they saw at once what they were.

"Presents!" said Snowstar excitedly. "I wonder where they came from?"

"This one is addressed to Pearl," said Emily, picking up the green-wrapped present.

"Our mermaid friend!" said Aisha.

But as Emily looked closer at the present,

the wrapping paper fell apart in her
hands, and the present dropped out. It was
a pair of very long socks, the colour of
mud.

"Socks?" said Snowstar, frowning. "For a
mermaid? That's not a very good present

at all!"

"It's Selena's horrible magic again," muttered Snowstar. "It's making the presents awful!"

"Help! Help me, please!" A little voice was squeaking from somewhere beneath them.

"Oh, candy canes!" gasped Snowstar. "I think someone's stuck under all this snow!"

# Chapter Four
# The Present Machine

Quickly the girls began to dig, scooping the snow with their mittens and doing their best to ignore the gusts of snowflakes whirling all around. Snowstar helped too, using his front hooves to pull away chunks of ice.

"I can see a hand!" cried Aisha

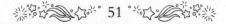

suddenly. She grabbed hold of it and tugged hard.

*Whoosh!* A little figure came shooting out of the snow and landed on its bottom.

The girls stared in amazement. It was a very small person, with long pointed ears and spiky white hair, dressed in a glittery silver tunic. She brushed snow off her

clothes. "Th-th-th-thank y-y-you!" she stammered. Her teeth were chattering with cold.

"It's Jolly!" cried Snowstar.

The unicorn

foal lowered his head and nuzzled Jolly, who flung her arms around Snowstar's nose and hugged him tight. "Phew!" she gasped. "S–S–Snowstar!"

"You know each other?" Emily said with wonder.

"Oh yes," said Snowstar. "Jolly is my best friend! She's one of the elves who make presents for the Winter Festival."

"I was looking for h–help when I got stuck in the snow," said Jolly. She looked a bit warmer now, after her hug with Snowstar, but her teeth were still chattering.

The girls looked at each other. They knew they needed to get the lockets back, but they couldn't ignore someone who

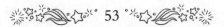

needed them. "We'll help you, Jolly," said Emily. "What's happened?"

"Ooh, thank you!" cried Jolly. She leapt to her feet, beaming happily. "Come on, I'll show you."

Just beyond the next snowdrift, they came to a large cabin built out of wooden logs. The windows shone with a warm yellow glow, and a string of coloured fairy lights hung along the edge

of the snow-covered roof. Jolly hopped off Snowstar and pushed open the door. It had a bushy green wreath on it, tied with a red satin bow.

"This is the elf workshop," Jolly told them, opening the door. The girls dusted snow from their mittens and stamped their boots. It was warm and cosy inside. What a relief to be out of the cold and howling winds!

Then they looked around and saw a huge, brightly coloured machine chugging and whirring in the middle of the cabin. It had cogs and levers and pipes that belched out steam, and a conveyor belt ran out of it and into another room. As the girls watched, the machine pumped out a toy train with a football at the front instead of an engine,

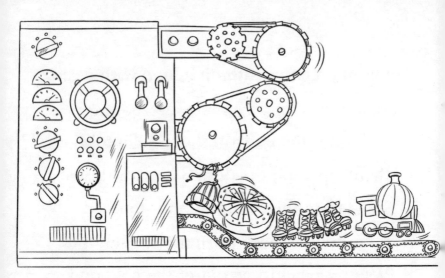

then three pairs of rollerblades made of
fudge, an inflatable dartboard and a pink
woolly hat that unravelled and got stuck
between two cogs.

Elves ran here and there with spanners
and screwdrivers, trying to fix the
machine. But everything they did just
seemed to make it worse.

"It's supposed to make lovely presents,"
wailed Jolly. "But then a few minutes

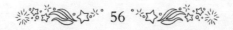

ago, a necklace came flying through the window and suddenly everything started to go wrong! These presents are all awful!"

The girls gasped.

"That must have been the Winter Presents locket!" said Emily.

"Do you know where the locket is now, Jolly?" Aisha asked.

Jolly shook her head. "It got lost in all the chaos."

Just then, yelps and wails came from the room next door.

"That's the wrapping room," said Jolly.

The elf led the way, following the conveyor belt. In the small room beyond, elves were falling all over the place,

struggling with large sheets of wrapping
paper. They were trying to wrap presents,
but instead the colourful paper seemed
to be wrapping itself. And the paper was
wrapping everything in sight. Even the
elves themselves were getting bundled up
in shiny, festive paper.

The girls hurried over and helped to
unwrap the elves.

"We need to find the locket and fix this
mess," said Emily when they'd finished.

Aisha gazed all around. Then she
spotted a little white creature zooming
along on the conveyor belt. "It's Blizz!"
she said, pointing. "Selena's naughty fox."

"Lots of presents, all for me!" Blizz was
muttering. He licked his lips. "Ooh, I

spy a chocolate teapot! Yummy …" He
scampered across the conveyor belt and
started stuffing pawfuls of chocolate into
his face.

But the girls saw something else in the
fox's paw too. Something that glittered
like ice …

"The locket!" said Emily.

"Let's catch him!" said Snowstar. He
galloped towards Blizz.

"Eek!" squealed the little white fox.
Dropping the teapot, he darted off, racing

around the workshop.

Aisha ran at the fox, and he switched direction. But now he was heading straight towards Snowstar, who lowered his horn.

Blizz skidded to a halt. "You'll never get the locket!" he yelped. Then he threw it high into the air …

"Catch it!" called Emily.

Aisha leaped for it, but it was

too high. Snowstar jumped too, swishing his tail. But instead of flying he just landed with a thump of his hooves.

"There it goes!" cried Jolly, as the locket flew into the room next door – the wrapping room. "Oh no … It's going to get wrapped!"

# Chapter Five
# A Silky Ribbon

Emily and Aisha dashed into the
wrapping room, with Jolly and Snowstar
hot on their heels.

"Uh-oh!" said Aisha.

The locket was nowhere to be seen.
Instead the room was piled high with
a mountain of badly wrapped presents.

Parcels covered the
floor, and in places
they almost touched
the ceiling.

"The locket must
have already been
wrapped," said Emily,
frowning.

"We'll have to
unwrap everything
to find it, then," said
Aisha.

The girls knelt on

the floor and began tearing the wrapping paper from the presents. Emily uncovered a broken doll, then a big lump of rock. Aisha ripped the paper from a wilted bouquet of flowers, then a rusty padlock with no key.

All the time, more presents were zooming in on the conveyor belt, and wrapping paper was magically covering them.

"It's no good," gasped Emily. "We can't unwrap them fast enough!"

A sheet of glittery silver paper swooped like an eagle towards Aisha, but Jolly fought it off with a long cardboard roll. "We'll protect you!" she called. She whistled, and elves dashed to form a circle

around the girls. They each clutched a
cardboard roll, ready to beat off any
paper that tried to wrap them up.

"Look!" cried Aisha suddenly.

Right at the top of the pile of presents,
one parcel was being wrapped over and
over, and it was growing bigger all the
time.

"Why's that one so special?" asked
Emily.

"Maybe it's the locket!" said Aisha.

Quickly the girls scrambled up the pile, gripping on to presents and hauling themselves higher. At last they reached the mysterious present. But as fast as they tore off bits of paper, more pieces came whooshing down to wrap it up again.

"We're getting nowhere!" panted Emily, as a fresh roll of star-speckled paper swept around the parcel.

"Watch out!" yelled Jolly.

The girls turned and saw that Blizz had darted in through the doorway.

"Naughty girls!" he squeaked when he spotted them. "I'll stop you!"

"Oh, candy canes!" wailed Snowstar. "If only I had magic, I could do something to help."

"Maybe you can do something!" said Emily. "You could use your horn to tear through the paper!"

"Do you really think so?" Snowstar's eyes shone with hope.

"It's worth a try," said Aisha. She and Emily gave the present a push. Down it rolled, bouncing and bumping over the mound of presents, until it stopped at Snowstar's hooves. The little foal took a deep breath. Then he plunged his horn down into the parcel, piercing through

every single piece of
wrapping paper.

*Clink!* Something
fell out on the floor.
The locket!

"It's mine!"
screeched Blizz.

"No, it's not!" yelled Aisha. She leapt
from the top of the presents, flew through
the air and landed – *thump!* – right by
the locket. She snatched it up, just as Blizz
was racing towards it.

"Noooo!" howled Blizz. He stamped
his paws. At once, a fresh roll of wrapping
paper flew down and wrapped him in
green and white stripy paper. Then a
ribbon whirled around his tummy and

tied itself into a beautiful purple bow.

"Awwww!" said Emily, giggling. "You look adorable."

"I'm not adorable!" Blizz squealed. He squirmed and wriggled until the wrapping paper fell off. Then he spotted the purple ribbon, and his eyes went wide. "Ooooh!" he yelped. "Look how silky it is!" He pounced, but the ribbon danced away. He crouched and pounced again. The ribbon kept on dancing, just out of reach.

"That should keep him busy for a

while!" said Aisha, grinning. Then she held up the glittering locket, and the little present inside turned gently, sparkling silver and green.

Suddenly the wonky presents finally stopped being wrapped, and the conveyor belt grinded to a halt.

"Woo hoo!" cried Jolly, punching the air. "You did it, girls! Thank you!"

The elves all cheered, waving their cardboard rolls in the air.

But one of the elves was pulling levers at the side of the conveyor belt. "It isn't working at all now," he said, looking puzzled.

"The nasty magic has stopped because we've taken the locket back from Selena," explained Snowstar. "But we still need to give it to my mum before it will work properly again."

"Where is Wintertail?" Jolly asked.

"Selena's kidnapped her!" Snowstar blinked back tears.

While several elves crowded round to comfort Snowstar, another elf darted to a little cupboard in the corner and brought back a large silver bag of toffees. He gave it to Emily and Aisha. "To say thank

you." He smiled
bashfully. "And
good luck."

"Thank you!"
said Emily, putting
the toffees into her
pocket.

"We'll need luck
to find the other
two lockets and
Wintertail so we can save Enchanted
Valley," said Aisha. She tucked the Winter
Presents locket into her snowsuit.

"Come on, then," said Emily. "What are
we waiting for?"

# STORY TWO

# WINTER SNOW

## Chapter Six
# The Magical Sleigh

"We've got no time to lose," said Aisha. "If we don't find the last two lockets and rescue Wintertail, the unicorns will have to make Selena queen of Enchanted Valley, or it'll keep snowing for ever!"

She threw open the door of the log cabin to reveal a snowdrift that was

almost higher than Snowstar's head!
Flurries still pelted down in thick white
sheets.

"Excuse me!" said a little voice.

The girls turned to see Jolly the elf
tugging at their snowsuits. Her pointed
ears quivered with excitement. "I think I
can help … Come on!"

Emily, Aisha and Snowstar followed her
out of the wrapping room and through a
door at the back of the cabin.

Outside, the air was freezing cold and
a chilly wind blew. Jolly hopped through
the snow to a small wooden shed. The
doors stood open, and the girls could see
something large, red and gleaming inside.

"Wow," said Aisha. "It's a sleigh!"

"It's beautiful," said Emily.

The sleigh was so shiny the girls could see their faces reflected in the red metal. It had silver runners, and the seats were covered in fluffy white padding.

"This is how we'll get through the snow!" said Jolly.

"Great idea!" said Snowstar. "We can head for Selena's castle to find my mum … and hopefully we'll find the other two lockets somewhere along the way."

Aisha frowned. "I don't understand. There aren't any reindeer to pull it!"

"This sleigh doesn't need reindeer," said Snowstar. "It's magical … It drives itself!"

"Perfect!" said Emily, clapping her hands together. "But are you sure you want to come too, Jolly? It might be dangerous."

"Just try to stop me!" said Jolly, nodding determinedly. "You helped us elves. Now it's my turn to help you."

The girls climbed into the front seat of the sleigh, while Jolly and Snowstar squeezed into the back seat. The fluffy white padding was even more comfy than it looked, and heated too; they could feel it through their snowsuits. There were presents piled up in the back of the sleigh but they all looked wonky and badly wrapped – and they wouldn't be fixed until Wintertail had her lockets again.

"Ready?" said Jolly. The girls nodded. There was a silver handrail, and they held on tight. "Then off we go!"

*Whoooooosh!* All of a sudden, the sleigh leapt forward. The girls lurched back in their seats as they shot off through the open doors, sliding across the snow.

"Woohoo!" cried Snowstar. "This is amazing."

The girls grinned at each other. Snowstar was right! They could feel the cold wind battering their faces, hurling snowflakes at them and tangling their

hair as they raced up and down the
snowdrifts, going faster and faster.

"It's like being in a speedboat!" said
Aisha.

They flashed past a cluster of little
gnome houses covered in snow, then a
lake, frozen like a mirror. All the while
the snow kept falling, getting heavier and
heavier.

The girls remembered Aurora's
directions – Selena's castle lay to the

west, just beyond the mountains. And sure
enough, in the distance they saw a dark
building looming over the snow, with tall,
twisted black turrets. Dark storm clouds
gathered above it, and they could see
lightning crackling down from the sky.

"It looks horrible!" said Aisha. "Just the
sort of place where Selena would live."

"We must hurry. My mum's in there!"
Snowstar cried.

"We've got to get over these mountains

first," said Jolly. "Hang on tight!"

The sleigh charged up the side of the first mountain. The girls clung to the handrail and huddled together. Snow swirled in their faces, and they bounced up and down as the sleigh struggled on through heavy snowdrifts. It was getting colder, and they seemed to be going slower the higher they got.

"The blizzard's getting worse!" called Snowstar, over the howl of the icy wind.

"And the s-s-snow's so d-d-deep!" cried Jolly. The poor little elf was shivering again.

The sleigh juddered on, but halfway up the mountain, it finally came to a halt.

"We'll have to go on foot," said Aisha,

trying to sound brave.

They all clambered out of the sleigh. Jolly hopped on to Snowstar's back and nestled into his mane for warmth. Even in their snowsuits, the girls felt chilly. But they set off, sinking into the snow with each step.

"This is hard work!" gasped Emily.

"If we can just get to the top—" Aisha began.

But before she could finish, the sky darkened above the summit, and there was a crackle and a flash of light. *BOOOOM!* Lightning forked from the clouds and struck the mountaintop.

There was a distant rumbling sound. At first the girls thought it must be thunder.

Then their hearts sank as they saw the snow shifting up above.

"Oh no," said Emily. "Avalanche!"

"Run!" cried Snowstar, his eyes wide with terror.

But there was no time.

*Whooooosh!* Down came the snow, like a tidal wave. It swept the girls off their feet and rushed on, carrying them back down the slopes.

## Chapter Seven
# Stuck

Emily and Aisha went head over heels,
tumbling down the mountainside.

"Help!" yelled Emily.

Then – *whumph!* – they landed at last
in a big snowdrift. Aisha's head poked up
just above the snow. She tugged her arms
free, but she couldn't pull herself out. "The

snow's packed in too tight!" she said.

Emily was just as stuck as Aisha. "Where are Jolly and Snowstar?" she wondered.

"H-h-here!" cried a little voice. The girls saw the elf buried even deeper in the snow, with just her face poking out. Her tiny nose was red with cold. "I c-can't get out!" she wailed.

Just then, Aisha spotted Snowstar

 wriggling out of the snow. The little foal clambered to his hooves and shook snow from his mane. "Oof!"

he gasped. "Oh dear, you're all still stuck.
Hold on, I think I have an idea!"

Quickly he galloped across the
mountainside to the sleigh. Emily and
Aisha could just see a sliver of it poking
out of a snowdrift. It was half buried,
and the presents had all spilled out of the
back.

"Maybe one of the presents could help,"
Snowstar said. He pulled out present after
present. "A broken wristwatch – useless!"
he called. "Some ugly, lumpy, grey cloaks
– no one would want to wear these!"

"Keep looking, Snowstar!" called Emily.

"You'll find something," Aisha added.

"Aha!" said Snowstar. He came trotting
over with a sludge-green scarf in his teeth.

"We can use this as a rescue rope," said
Snowstar when he'd dropped it on the
ground.

"Great idea!" said Aisha.

The foal dipped his head, and Emily
looped the rope around his body. Then
Emily and Aisha each took one end of
the scarf. Snowstar trotted backwards
until the scarf was taut. He dug his hooves
in and began to pull.

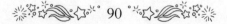

"You can do it, Snowstar!" called Jolly.

"I think I'm moving!" cried Aisha.

Snowstar heaved and heaved … then suddenly the girls shot out like corks popping from a bottle. Snowstar stumbled forward, panting. "I did it!" he gasped. "I can't believe it!"

"Hooray!" cheered the girls. They ran to give Snowstar a quick hug. Then together they darted over to Jolly and dug the little elf free from the snow.

"Phew!" said Jolly, brushing snow from her silver tunic, as Aisha set her down on the ground. "All this excitement has warmed me up a bit!"

They put the scarf back in the sleigh, then set off, climbing the mountain again.

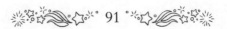

But they hadn't gone far when something went *swish* through the air nearby.

"What was that?" gasped Snowstar.

"I think it was a snowball!" said Jolly.

*Swish! Swish!* Two more snowballs flew past them.

"They came from over there," said Emily, pointing to a big rock covered with snow. Suddenly a little white figure darted out from behind it and hurled another snowball, which only just missed Jolly.

"Uh-oh!" cried Aisha. "It's Blizz!"

## Chapter Eight
# The Icy Cavern

"Yaaah!" yelled Blizz, sticking his tongue out. "Prepare to get snowballed!"

He tossed another pawful of snow, and it splattered against Aisha's shoulder. Aisha took a step back, and a chain fell out of her pocket. "Whoa," she gasped, stuffing it back inside. "That's the Winter Presents locket. We mustn't lose it!"

Blizz threw another snowball, and
Emily skipped out of the way. "That one
nearly hit me in the face!" she cried.

"Yikes!" said Jolly, crouching down
behind a mound of snow.

The girls and Snowstar joined her.

"If Blizz is here, maybe one of the
lockets is nearby too," Aisha mused.

"You might be right," said Emily. "The
snow is much thicker here than anywhere
else. Remember when we were looking
for the Nature lockets?"

"Yes," said Aisha. "The problem was
always much worse wherever the locket
was."

"Exactly. This could be the same – we

might be near the Winter Snow locket!"
Emily said.

"So, what do we do?" Jolly asked. "How can we get rid of Blizz long enough to search for it?"

Snowstar stomped his hoof crossly. "I say if he wants a snowball fight, we should give him one!"

"Agreed!" said Aisha. She scooped up some snow and threw it back at Blizz. The snowball flew straight and true. "Take that!"

Emily and Jolly joined in, and soon all three of them were pelting Blizz with snowballs. There were so many that the little fox had to hide behind his rock again. "Not fair!" he whined. "Three against one!"

"Quick," whispered Emily. "Let's go and search for the locket while he's hiding!"

The girls sneaked off with Snowstar, leaving Jolly to throw a few more snowballs before she came scampering after them.

Before long, they had left Blizz far behind. The ground got steeper as they got higher, and soon they were close to the top of the mountain. But something wasn't quite right.

"I don't understand," said Aisha. "The snow isn't falling so hard here."

"You don't think we've gone past the locket, do you?" wondered Emily.

Suddenly Jolly the little elf yelled out

from behind them, "Whoa!"

The girls whirled round. Snowstar was there, but the elf was nowhere to be seen.

"Jolly's vanished!" gasped Snowstar.

Emily and Aisha scrambled back to where they'd last seen Jolly. There, just behind a big pile of snow, was a dark, gaping hole. Aisha bent down over it.

"Are you in there, Jolly?" she called.

"Yes – I fell in!" came the elf's voice from below. "I'm OK, though … and I think I can see the locket!"

Emily and Aisha

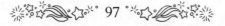

exchanged a glance.

"Should we go down there?" asked Snowstar nervously.

"We'll have to!" said Aisha. "Don't worry, though – we'll help you."

The girls held on tight to Snowstar as he lowered his hooves into the hole. Then they let go, and the foal leapt down. *Thump!* They heard his hooves hit the ice below.

Aisha went next, sliding down and landing in a crouch. Emily followed, but when her boots hit the ground she slipped and fell with a bump on to her bottom. A tinkling sound rang out, and a few icicles dropped and shattered on the ground close to the girls' boots.

Emily picked up one of the fallen icicles with a shaking hand. "Look how sharp it is!" she said nervously.

The girls looked around. They were standing in a large, icy cavern. There were icicles everywhere, dangling from the ceiling and spearing up from the rocky ground. Each one was very long, so they had to duck down carefully to avoid hitting them.

Here and there, blue crystals glittered among the rocks of the ceiling, throwing an eerie sapphire light through the darkness. It was cold and silent all around.

"Those are icelights," whispered Snowstar. His voice echoed in the cavern. "They only glow when it's really cold."

"Where did you see the locket, Jolly?" asked Aisha.

Jolly pointed to the far end of the

cavern. High up, twinkling near the
ceiling, was a little crystal locket. It
dangled in mid-air, with the end of the
chain frozen within an icicle.

"There it is!" whinnied Snowstar, tossing
his mane happily.

Emily frowned. "But look at all the
icicles in the way. How are we going to
get to the locket without getting hurt?"

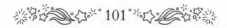

## Chapter Nine
# The Leaping Unicorn

The girls set out, stepping carefully on the bumpy, icy ground. They had to crouch and zigzag to squeeze through the forest of icicles.

"I don't like this," muttered Snowstar, from behind. He had to pick his hooves up high so as not to break off any ice.

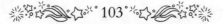

The further in they went, the more the spiky icicles clustered together. Once the girls reached a solid wall of icicles, and they had to go back to find another way.

"It's like a maze," said Emily. "And we're only halfway through!"

Suddenly Snowstar gave a panicked neigh.

The little foal was slipping on the ice. Skidding, he staggered into a low-hanging icicle. *Crack!* It snapped, and a strange tinkling noise sounded again throughout the cavern.

"Look out!" yelled Aisha.

The girls and Jolly ducked, throwing their arms over their heads.

A moment later more icicles cracked

and fell from the
ceiling. *Crash!*
*Crunch!* They
exploded all
around in little
bursts of icy spray.

"Whoa!" cried
Jolly, as one
shattered by her foot. "That was close!"

Everyone stayed completely still, until
the tinkling had died away and the
cavern was silent. Then they began to
pick their way through the icicles again.

At last they clambered over a mound
of rocks and stood beneath the locket.
"It's higher than I thought," said Emily,
staring anxiously at it. She stood on

tiptoes and reached up as far as she could, but she couldn't even get close to it.

"Maybe if I stood on your shoulders," said Jolly.

Aisha lifted the little elf and settled her behind her head. Jolly stretched and stretched, but she barely got any closer than Emily had.

"Oh dear," said Snowstar sadly. "If only I could fly …"

"That gives me an idea!" said Emily. "Maybe you can't fly, but I bet you can jump higher than any of us."

"Really?" Snowstar seemed doubtful.

"I'm sure you can!" said Aisha. "Especially with a run-up. You could jump off that mound of rocks over there."

Snowstar peered at the rocks then nodded bravely. "All right. I'll give it a try!"

The little foal tip-hooved through the icicles until he was behind the rocks. Then he snorted with determination. He set off, trotting at first. Then he began to canter … then gallop … The cavern trembled with his hoofbeats, and the girls and Jolly ducked for cover as some smaller icicles crashed down from the ceiling.

"Go, Snowstar!" they shouted.

Snowstar galloped right up on to the

rocks. Then he reached out with his
hooves and pushed off as hard as he
could. He flew through the air, his mane
and tail streaming, his neck stretching.

"Yes!" cried Aisha.

*Crrrrrack!* Snowstar struck the icicle
with his horn, and it snapped off. Down
it fell, the locket glinting. Aisha dived and
caught the precious locket in both hands,
just as Snowstar landed and skidded to a

halt on all four hooves.

Emily and Jolly leapt to their feet, cheering. "Hooray! You did it!"

## Chapter Ten
# Something Fishy

"Well done, Snowstar!" said Emily, stroking his flank.

Aisha pulled the chain free from the broken icicle and hung it carefully around Snowstar's neck. Inside the locket, the tiny snowflake glittered.

Just then, a furry white creature leaped

down into the cavern. The girls' hearts sank when they saw who it was.

"That's mine!" screeched Blizz, swishing his bushy tail crossly. "Give it back!"

The fox darted towards them. Light and fast, he weaved in and out of the icicles, which hardly slowed him down at all.

"Back off, Blizz!" Emily shouted. She and Aisha moved to step in front of Snowstar to protect him and the locket, but it was too late. Snowstar's hooves scrabbled over the ice as the foal turned and galloped away in a panic.

"Look out!" cried Jolly, pointing to a dark area on the ground.

Unable to stop, Snowstar hit the patch of black ice. His legs skidded away, and

he thumped into the wall of the cavern.
*Clink!* The locket flew from his neck and
landed on the ice.

"Oh no!" gasped Emily

Quick as a flash, Blizz darted over,
snatched the chain in his teeth and
flipped it on to his own neck, cackling
in triumph. "Got it!" he crowed. "I'm too
clever for you! Now Selena is sure to let
me join her feast!"

"What feast?" said Jolly to the others,

frowning in confusion.

"I don't know," said Emily. She lowered her voice to a whisper. "But it gives me an idea! Do you remember how Blizz ate all those roasted chestnuts at the Winter Festival?"

"And that chocolate teapot in the elves' cabin!" added Aisha.

"He's really greedy!" said Emily. "And look what I've got." She reached into her pocket and pulled out the bag of sticky toffees that the elves had given them. "We can distract him with these, then grab the locket!"

"Great idea!" said Aisha. She cleared her throat. "Mmmm, yummy toffees!" she said loudly. "I hope no one else wants one!"

Blizz froze. His ears pricked up. The girls saw that he was staring at the bag of toffees now, with his tongue hanging out.

"I'll have one!" said Emily. She pretended to put one in her mouth. "Wow, it's the best toffee ever!"

"Save some for me!" said Jolly, as loudly as she could. "Ooh, they're nearly all gone …"

"Stop!" yelled Blizz. "I want one!"

The little fox scurried over the ice towards them. Aisha lowered the bag, and Blizz thrust his paw inside and stuffed a toffee into his mouth. He began to chew.

"It'th very thticky!" he said. "And it tathtes of fith!"

Jolly scratched her head. "What's fith?" she wondered.

"I think he means fish!" whispered Emily. "That's strange."

"Oh!" said Jolly. "I forgot to say. They're magical toffees. They taste just like your favourite flavour."

Aisha wrinkled her nose. "Blizz's favourite toffee flavour is fish?!"

Blizz wasn't listening. His eyes widened as he scooped up more toffees and shoved them into his mouth. "Very, very tathty!"

Carefully, quietly, Aisha reached around Blizz's neck. She lifted the chain, then whipped it off. Blizz was far too busy

chomping away to notice. He didn't even
notice when Snowstar, Jolly and the girls
crept away.

In no time at all they had clambered up
out of the cavern, back into the cold air
and the snow. Aisha and Emily grinned at
each other.

"The snow's stopped falling!" said Aisha.

"The blizzard's gone!" added Emily. "It

must be because we found the locket."

But there was still a thick, heavy blanket of whiteness across the ground, and the girls knew that it wouldn't go away until they found Wintertail.

As they set off down the slopes of the mountain, Aisha tucked the Winter Snow locket into her snowsuit, next to the Winter Presents one. The air had cleared and they could see Selena's castle now. It stood ahead of them, black as night against the pure white snow.

"I don't like the thought of going in there," said Jolly anxiously.

"Don't be afraid," said Emily, throwing an arm around the elf. "We'll be fine if we stick together."

"That's right," said Aisha with determination. "Besides, Wintertail is in there … and she's counting on us!"

## STORY THREE

## WINTER FEAST

## Chapter Eleven
# Grumpy Trolls

Emily and Aisha held on tight to the sides as the shiny red sleigh shot across the snow. In the seats in front of them, Jolly the elf snuggled up close to the young unicorn Snowstar.

Aisha could feel the two lockets they had already found bouncing in her

pocket. There
was only one
more to track
down – the
Winter Feast
locket – and perhaps Wintertail would
know where to find it.

The wind tangled the girls' hair and
forced them to squint. They could see
forests and rivers rushing past on each
side, as the sleigh carried them up and
down the snowdrifts like a boat on a
stormy sea.

"The snow's still so deep!" cried Emily,
over the wailing of the wind.

Aisha nodded. "The whole valley is
completely buried."

In front of them, Snowstar whimpered, "If we don't save my mum soon, Queen Aurora will have to surrender to save the kingdom!"

"Then Selena will be queen of the valley!" added Jolly. The little elf shuddered in horror at the thought.

"Don't worry," said Aisha. "We won't let that happen."

The sleigh swooped to the top of another snowdrift. Selena's castle was much closer now. It loomed against the white sky, like a horrible black mountain. Storm clouds raged above the jagged turrets, and black banners hung from the walls with silver lightning bolts on them.

Jolly tapped the handrail, and the

sleigh swerved behind a big snowy rock.
Everyone jumped off, then they took it in
turns to peep out from behind the rock.
Aisha saw grumpy-looking creatures
stomping in and out of the castle,
carrying plates and cutlery. They had
little black eyes and tufty hair, and they
all wore grey uniforms.

"Trolls!" gasped Jolly.

"There are so many of them," said
Emily anxiously. "How are we going to

get in without them seeing us?"

"They look really busy," said Aisha. "If we were as lumpy and grey as they were, maybe they wouldn't notice us?"

Emily thought for a moment. "Those ugly grey, lumpy cloaks Snowstar found in the sleigh! We can use them to disguise ourselves!"

The friends went to the back of the sleigh and dug out the grey cloaks they'd seen earlier. They helped each other to fasten the clasps around their necks.

Aisha giggled as she pulled the hood over her hair. "We look just like trolls!"

They snuck over to the castle gate. It was a big, black metal door with heavy studs all around and it was still open because of all the trolls coming in and out.

"I hope this works!" said Emily.

They stepped inside and found themselves in a low stone corridor. Arched doorways ran along each wall, and at the end of the corridor a set of wide stone steps disappeared up into darkness.

"This place is horrible!" said Snowstar, flicking his tail nervously.

"Which way do we go?" wondered Aisha.

But before they could decide, a large troll came bustling out of an archway carrying a clipboard. He stopped and squinted at them with his piggy eyes.

They held their breath …

"Oi!" grunted the troll. "You lot are late for work!" He stopped and frowned at Snowstar. "Never seen a troll with four legs before."

"He's a uni-troll," said Emily quickly.

The troll scowled. "I don't care what he is!" He pointed to the largest of the archways. "Into the kitchens!"

"But—" began Aisha.

"Now!" roared the troll. He swept an

armful of aprons from a set of pegs and bundled them into Aisha's arms. "Quick march, on the double!"

It seemed they'd got away with it. But how long would it be before one of the trolls noticed that they were intruders in Selena's castle?

## Chapter Twelve
# Sleepy Stew

The troll hustled them through the archway, and the girls found themselves in a big, bustling kitchen. It was full of trolls in aprons. There was a warm, cosy fire burning in the hearth – but everything else about it was horrid. A row of pots, blackened with soot and crusted with grime, was set over the fire. A big wooden table ran down the middle of the kitchen. It was coated in thick dust and laden with disgusting food.

"Yuck!" whispered Emily, as she took in the squashed old sandwiches, a pot of murky grey soup and a green cake decorated with spiders. "How are we

going to get out of here? We'll never find Wintertail if we're stuck in the kitchen."

"Don't just stand there!" grunted the troll.

He pointed at Snowstar. "You! We need more mud flavouring for the brownies. And you!" He shoved Jolly towards the fire. "Stir the sludge stew, so it doesn't stick."

While Snowstar trotted to a store cupboard – hiding his face under his cloak as best he could – Jolly took a cracked old wooden spoon from a dirty jug and reached for the nearest pot.

"NOT THAT ONE!" roared the troll, so loudly that Jolly leapt a metre into the air. "That's the sleeping potion,

mud-for-brains!"

"Sleeping potion?" said Emily, frowning.

"That's what I said, rocks-for-ears,"
growled the troll. "It's only for the
prisoner in the tallest tower." He pointed
to another pot. "That one is the sludge
stew. Now hop to it!"

As the troll hurried off, shaking his head
and grumbling, Emily and Aisha shared a
glance.

"A prisoner in the tallest tower …" said
Aisha.

"It must be Wintertail!" said Emily.

"OI!" shouted the troll, from over by the
table. "You two, follow me!"

The girls hurried over.

"Take these dishes to the dining room,"

said the troll, waving a hand at the food on the table. He never looked at their faces. "Don't keep her highness waiting!"

"We'll be back as soon as we can," Emily told Jolly and Snowstar. Then she grabbed a bowl of furry-looking biscuits, while Aisha picked up a pizza that was topped with pebbles. They joined a crew of trolls who were already ferrying dishes out of the kitchen.

The girls kept their heads down as they followed the trolls through a side door and into a dining room. It was even bigger than the kitchen and much emptier. A few dusty oil paintings of Selena in different poses hung on the black walls. Another long table stood on

the cold flagstones, with a filthy grey
tablecloth draped over it. Only one diner
sat at the very end of the table.

"It's her!" gasped Emily. "It's Selena!"

The evil unicorn was snorting and
gobbling down plate after plate of food.
She was eating so fast that each troll had
to take away an empty plate for every
one they set down.

"More food!" Selena roared. "This is the best Winter Festival ever, and it's all for me!" she cackled. "No rotten roast chestnuts! No sloppy snowcones! My food is a thousand times better!"

As the girls got closer, they saw something around Selena's neck, glinting in the light of the dusty old chandelier that hung from the ceiling.

"It's the Winter Feast locket!" whispered Aisha. They could see the sparkling little candy cane inside.

"How on earth are we going to get it back?" sighed Emily.

Just then, the girls saw a furry little white creature slink into the room from a side door. Blizz darted over to the table, hopped up and reached for a stale crisp. But Selena knocked his paw away with a hoof. "You useless thing!" she snapped. "You've already lost two lockets. You don't deserve any food!"

Blizz whined and tucked his tail between his legs. Then he hopped off the table and scampered away.

It was the girls' turn to serve. Quickly they set the plates down and moved on, worried that Selena would recognise

them. But the unicorn was too busy guzzling a dish of rotten vegetables to notice them at all.

Aisha frowned as they headed back to the kitchen. "Emily," she whispered. "I think I've got an idea …"

A short while later, they were back at the kitchen table. Emily winked at Aisha, then pushed a plate of soggy cabbage off the edge. *SPLAT!* It sploshed across the floor.

"Oops!" cried out Emily. "What a silly troll I am!"

The troll who'd given them the aprons charged over, muttering angrily, his eyes only on the mess. "What do you think

you're doing now?"

While he was grumbling at Emily, Aisha scurried over to the sludge stew, where Jolly was still stirring away. Aisha put a finger to her lips then borrowed Jolly's spoon and scooped out some of the sleeping potion. It was bright green and bubbled gently. She slipped it straight into the pot of sludge stew, and gave the spoon back to Jolly. "Shh!" she whispered to the elf, who gave a thumbs-up. Then she took the pot of stew.

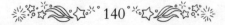

The head troll was still scolding Emily. "… supposed to be helping, not chucking food around."

"Excuse me, sir," said Aisha, bowing her head so the troll wouldn't see her properly. "I need this troll to help me carry this. We mustn't keep Her Highness waiting!"

The troll scowled. "Off you go, then."

Emily ran over, and together they

carried the pot of stew to the dining room.

Selena was slumped on her throne, with empty plates piled up all around her. When the girls set the pot down in front of her, she waved it away with a hoof. "I told the others already! I've had enough."

"Um – you really should try it, Your Highness," said Emily in a grumbly voice, trying to sound as trollish as possible. "It's the, um, best dish!"

"It's famous in Troll Land," added Aisha. "For being the stinkiest, slimiest stew of all."

Selena's ears pricked up. "Stinky and slimy, you say? Oh well, if you insist."

She dipped her head in the pot, slurping

up the stew.

"It worked!" whispered Emily. "Pretty soon she's going to be—"

*Thump!* Before Emily could finish her sentence, Selena's head hit the table. Her eyes closed, and she began to snore loudly.

# Chapter Thirteen
# Magic at Last

Aisha reached around Selena's neck, trying not to touch the silver unicorn. She undid the clasp at the back of the chain. But just as she was lifting the pendant free, Selena snorted.

The girls froze. Selena blinked. She shifted her head. Then she mumbled something under her breath and her eyes closed. At last she began to snore again.

"Phew!" gasped Aisha. "Let's get out of here. We don't know how long the potion lasts!"

The girls hurried out of the dining room, as fast as they could.

In the kitchen, they found plenty of trolls still bustling around preparing food. The head troll was hovering by the door, giving out orders and waving a wooden spoon at anyone who was working too slowly. Snowstar was fetching ingredients, and Jolly was stuck by the fire, stirring more horrible stews and soups.

The girls darted through the kitchen to join the little elf.

"Did you get it?" asked Jolly.

Aisha quickly showed her the pendant. Then she tucked it away in her pocket for safekeeping.

"What now?" wondered Emily.

"We need to find Wintertail," said Aisha.

"But how?" said Emily. "We'd be lucky to get past that horrible troll with the spoon, let alone all the others!"

"I know how we can get out of here," said Jolly thoughtfully. And before the girls could say anything more, Jolly hopped up on the kitchen table and whipped off her cloak.

"Hey, everyone!" called Jolly, jumping up and down. "Surprise! I'm an elf! And I stole Queen Selena's locket, so ha-ha!"

The kitchen fell silent. For a moment the trolls just stared at Jolly, blinking their tiny black eyes in disbelief. Then the head troll growled and pointed his spoon at her. "Catch that little rotter!"

Every troll in the kitchen lurched towards Jolly. The elf dived off the table, ducked between the head troll's legs and slipped out the door. But the trolls followed, squashing and squeezing through the doorway, all shoving at one

another to be the first to catch her.

"Sound the alarm!" they roared. "Get the elf! She's stolen from the queen!"

Emily, Aisha and Snowstar hurried over to a tiny window. Crowding round to peer through the smudged glass, they saw Jolly tear across the snow and jump into the sleigh. It shot off, just as the first trolls were starting to catch up with her.

"She's so brave!" gasped Snowstar.

"Come on," said Emily. "Let's find your mum!"

The three of them ran out of the kitchen and hurried up the stairs. They wound round in a spiral, going higher and higher. There were no windows, and the walls and ceilings were black, but

flaming torches lit the way.

At last they came to a big wooden door with a heavy bolt across it. Aisha slid the bolt back, and Emily pushed it open with a loud *creeeeak!*

Hearts racing, they stepped inside.

It was a small, round room with a stone floor and no furniture – just a single window to let in daylight. And lying on her side in the middle of the room, snoring softly, was a large white unicorn.

"Mum!" cried Snowstar. The foal dashed over and nuzzled her with his soft black nose. But Wintertail didn't move.

The girls ran over and knelt at Wintertail's side. They stroked her mane, but the unicorn still didn't stir.

 150

"Oh dear," muttered Aisha. "We can't possibly carry her."

Snowstar's ears drooped. His head fell and he began to cry, his tears splashing on to Wintertail's nose. "I wish she'd wake up," he mumbled. "I miss her!"

"Poor Snowstar!" said Aisha.

The girls were just about to hug Snowstar when something strange

happened. Silver sparkles swirled around him, like a flurry of ice crystals. Then his horn began to glow. Lights shimmered around it in a wash of colours – bright reds, greens and blues.

"Oh wow!" gasped Emily.

"It's beautiful!" whispered Aisha.

Snowstar's tear-filled eyes grew wide. "What's happening?"

The girls grinned.

"I think you've got your magic at last,"
said Emily. "And look! It's waking your
mum!"

The silver sparkles were swirling
faster now, circling Wintertail as well
as Snowstar. The white unicorn's tail
swished. Then one hoof twitched.

Wintertail's eyelids fluttered, then
blinked open. She lifted her head, looking
round in a daze.

"Mum!" cried Snowstar.

"Snowstar!" said Wintertail.

Snowstar shook his mane with
excitement. "I can't believe it," he
whinnied. "I found you! And I got my
magic! I'm so happy I could... I could..."

The girls stared in astonishment.

Snowstar was floating up from the ground! Slowly the foal rose through the air, his hooves trailing silver sparkles. He gasped. "I'm flying!" He flicked his tail, and he whooshed around the room in a circle.

"My little Snowstar!" cried Wintertail.

"Not so 'little' any more," laughed Emily in delight.

The girls clapped and cheered.

Wintertail turned her big white head towards them and smiled, her blue eyes twinkling. "Why, it's Emily and Aisha!" she said. "You came to rescue me!"

"That's not all," said Emily. "We found your lockets."

Aisha pulled the three lockets from her pocket and carefully hung them around Wintertail's neck. But just as she stepped back, the girls heard something coming up the stairs. It sounded like hoofbeats, thundering in a gallop, closer and closer …

"Uh-oh," said Aisha. "It's Selena. She's awake!"

## Chapter Fourteen
# Through the Window

*Bang!* The door flew open and hit the wall.

Selena charged in, her silver coat fizzing and crackling with electricity. Her purple eyes blazed with fury, and she snorted and stamped her hooves. Blizz came scampering after her, his head lowered, his

tail between his legs.

"Meddling girls!" roared Selena. "Those lockets are mine! Give them back, right now!"

"Never!" said Emily.

"And they're not yours," said Aisha, standing beside Emily. "They belong to Wintertail!"

Selena narrowed her eyes. "Very well, then … If you won't give them to me, I'll take them for myself!"

*Ffffzzzzapp!* A lightning bolt sparked

from her horn. The girls ducked, holding tight to Wintertail. *Crrrrack!* The lightning struck the wall and scorched the stones black.

"You missed!" called Snowstar, hovering above. "Better luck next time!"

Selena snarled. *Ffzzapp! Fffzzzappp! Ffffzzzzappp!* More bolts shot from her horn, lighting the room up with flashes of white. The girls had to dodge again and again.

"The window!" called Aisha. She ran across and pushed it open, and a gust of cold air blew into the room.

"I'll carry you," said Wintertail, rising shakily to her hooves.

Quickly the girls scrambled on to the

white unicorn's back. Aisha clung on to
Wintertail's mane. Emily sat behind her
and wrapped her arms around Aisha's
waist.

"Ready!" called both girls. Wintertail
set off, cantering towards the window.

"Come on, Snowstar!" yelled Emily.

The little foal flitted out of the way of
another lightning bolt – *Ffffzzapp!* – then
swooped out through the window.

*Whooosh!* Wintertail followed Snowstar, carrying the girls with her. The cold air rushed over them, and snowflakes blew in their faces, catching in their hair.

Aisha looked over her shoulder. Selena was charging across the room towards them. "Uh-oh!" she called. "She's coming after us!"

But Wintertail was already turning in mid-air. Her horn began to glow with an

icy blue light.

"Whoa!" gasped Emily, pointing.

Silver sparkles were swirling around
the window, and icicles were magically
growing across it. Up and down, left and
right, they covered the window like an icy
cage.

*Thump!* Selena leapt straight into the ice
and fell back into the room.

"She's trapped!" cried Aisha, punching
the air.

"Go,
Wintertail!"
said Emily.

Selena shook
her mane with
fury. Electricity

sparked across her silver coat. "This isn't over!" she howled. "You'll see!"

But there was nothing she could do. Wintertail swooped away through the falling snowflakes, with Snowstar flying beside her. Looking back, the girls saw Selena's castle getting smaller and smaller, until it looked no bigger than a doll's house in the distance.

"Look!" cried Aisha, pointing to the ground.

The girls watched in awe as Enchanted Valley began to change. The thick white snow was melting, like water draining from a bath. Soon there was just a light, pretty dusting, like powdered sugar. The wind died away, and the snowflakes

drifted quietly down, far fewer than
before.

"Wintertail's magic is working!" sighed
Emily happily. "And look – I can see
Jolly!"

There was the little red sleigh, racing
across a snowy field towards Aurora's
golden palace. At first the girls couldn't
see the trolls. Then Aisha spotted them,
trudging off in the opposite direction,
back towards Selena's castle.

"They've given up!" giggled Aisha.

They swooped down lower, until they could see the little elf riding in the sleigh, her spiky white hair blowing back in the breeze.

"Hello, Jolly!" called the girls.

The elf waved back at them. "Hello, girls!" She grinned. "The snow is all pretty again! You've done it! You've saved Enchanted Valley!"

## Chapter Fifteen
# Winter Lights

"Look!" cried Emily, as they flew over Aurora's golden palace. "I can see the Winter Festival!"

Everyone seemed to be having even more fun than before. As they flew lower, they swished through a crowd of laughing unicorns who were building

creatures out of snow. They swooped past trees shimmering with snowflakes, then swooshed around a brightly lit helter-skelter.

At last Wintertail's four hooves hit the snow, sinking in deep, and the girls hopped off her back.

At once a crowd gathered around them, led by Queen Aurora herself.

"Three cheers

for the saviours of Enchanted Valley!"
called Aurora. "Hip, hip …"

"Hooray!" cried all the unicorns.

"Thank you, girls," said Queen Aurora,
when the cheering had died down at last.
"You did it again!"

"Don't forget Snowstar and Jolly,"
said Emily. "We could never have done
it without them. And now the Winter

Festival is perfect."

"Almost perfect," said Wintertail sadly. She was looking at the strings of lights that hung from the trees around the festival. They were still out.

"Ah yes," said Aurora. "I'm afraid the lights were broken by one of Selena's lightning bolts. We haven't been able to mend them."

"Don't worry!" said a familiar voice.

The girls turned to see Snowstar flying down to land in the snow beside them. "We might not have twinkly lights," said the little foal. "But I can show you something much better!" He reared up on his hind legs, and his horn glowed with an icy light.

The girls gasped. High above, coloured lights began to glimmer. They lit up the whole sky, turning it red, then green and blue. The unicorns all gazed up in wonder, making oohs and aahs at the incredible display.

Wintertail nuzzled her son proudly, while Queen Aurora stared in astonishment. "Snowstar!" said Aurora.

"You have your magic! That means it's time for you to receive your magical locket."

The unicorn queen stepped across the snow and lowered her head, touching her horn to Snowstar's.

At once a cloud of gold and silver sparkles burst from the horns, swirling around them like a flurry of snowflakes.

For a moment the girls couldn't see either of the unicorns. Then the sparkles disappeared, and they saw that Snowstar had a locket hanging from a chain around his neck.

Emily peered closer. Inside the locket was a tiny silver star, surrounded by shimmering coloured lights.

"It's beautiful!" breathed Aisha. "What does it mean?"

"From now on," said Queen Aurora, "Snowstar's own special magic will

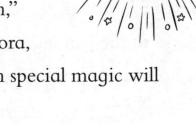

protect the Winter Lights."

The unicorns all cheered. Snowstar bashfully flicked his tail, his eyes shining with happiness.

Suddenly there was a spray of snow as the shiny red sleigh skidded to a halt nearby. Out hopped Jolly, followed by the other elves, all dusting snow from their clothes.

"I picked them up on the way!" said Jolly cheerfully. She pointed to a huge pile of shiny gifts in the back of the sleigh. "Come on, everyone. It's present time!"

Aurora and Wintertail trotted over to the sleigh, and together they passed out presents to the waiting unicorns.

"I hope there won't be any chocolate

teapots this time!" whispered Emily.

"Or inflatable dart boards!" added
Aisha.

But the air was soon filled with squeals
of joy and whoops of delight. There were
sparkly woolly hats, shiny new ice skates,
silky warm cloaks, colourful boxes of
candy … The presents were all perfect!

Out of the corner of her eye, Emily

spotted something behind the sleigh. It looked like a flash of white fur. "I see you, Blizz!" she called.

The little fox poked his black nose out and blinked at them.

Aisha put her hands on her hips. "If you're here to cause trouble, you'd better go right now," she said sternly.

Blizz shook his head. His eyes darted around nervously. "Actually …" he said, "I've had enough of helping Selena. She wouldn't let me have a single thing to eat! Even after everything I did for her."

"That's because she's really mean!" said Emily. "You shouldn't have listened to her."

"You're right, and I'm sorry," said Blizz.

He pawed sheepishly at the snow. "Please can I stay for the Winter Festival?"

"Of course you can," said Aisha, leaning down to stroke Blizz's head.

"Oh no, he can't!" said Wintertail. The girls turned in surprise to the white unicorn. But Wintertail's eyes were shining. "Not without a present, anyway!"

A little silver parcel magically appeared on the snow by Emily's feet, making Blizz gasp with delight.

The girls watched as

he ripped off the wrapping paper with his teeth. Inside was a golden box full of chocolates.

"Oh my …" said Blizz. "Thank you so much!" He looked up hopefully. "I don't suppose … are they fish flavour?"

Wintertail's eyes widened with surprise, but all the same she lowered her head and waved her horn over the box. It sparkled for an instant.

"They are now!" she said.

As Blizz began snuffling up chocolates, Wintertail turned to the girls. "Now it's time for your presents," she said. "Snowstar has chosen them especially for you."

The foal trotted over and lowered his horn. Two charms slid off it, landing neatly in the girls' hands. They held them up to catch the light. They were matching snowflakes, made of ice-white crystal.

"They're perfect," said both girls at the same time, as they added the charms to their keyrings.

"Now come on," said Snowstar, tossing his mane happily. "Let's enjoy the festival!"

The girls ate roast chestnuts from a paper

bag, then made snowmen with the elves. They rode a carousel with beautiful model penguins instead of horses. Finally they huddled close with Snowstar and Aurora, watching the last of the colourful lights dancing through the darkening sky.

"This has been the best Winter Festival ever!" said Snowstar with a happy sigh. "And it's thanks to you girls."

"Is it really over?" said Emily sadly.

Queen Aurora nodded. "I'm afraid so. It's time for you girls to go home. But don't worry … I have a feeling you'll be returning to Enchanted Valley very soon."

The unicorn queen lowered her horn, and a cloud of golden sparkles swirled out of thin air. The sparkles raced around

the girls, faster and faster, and Emily and
Aisha felt their feet leaving the ground …

✦ ✦

A moment later they floated down to
land on a crisp, frosty lawn.

They blinked, gazing all around. They
were back in the garden of Enchanted
Cottage, in the very spot they'd stood
when they had disappeared.

"What an adventure that was," said

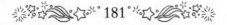

Aisha in wonder.

"And we even got to play in some snow!" said Emily.

Just then, something came drifting down between them. Aisha held out a hand and caught it. "A snowflake!" she gasped.

The girls looked up. Sure enough, more snowflakes were falling silently from the white sky.

"It's snowing!" cried Emily, punching the air. "I knew it would!"

"Girls!" called someone from inside.

They turned to see Mrs Khan leaning out of the window and grinning at them. "Who's for some nice hot cocoa?" she said.

"Yum!" said Aisha. "Thanks, Mum."

"There should be lots of snow by the time we get back out," said Emily, as they walked through the falling snowflakes to the back door.

"We can make a snowman!" said Aisha, thinking of the fun they'd had with the elves.

"Or even better …" said Emily, "a snow unicorn!"

The End

**Join Emily and Aisha
for another adventure in …**
## Silvermane Saves
## the Stars
**Read on for a sneak peek!**

Emily Turner gazed around in wonder. "Your garden looks even more magical at twilight!" she said.

Her best friend, Aisha Khan, grinned and spread a tartan blanket on the grass.

The moon shone like a new coin, and in the middle of the lawn, the stone statue of a phoenix gleamed against the deep blue sky. It looked as though it might take off at any moment.

"That's because of all this starlight!" said Aisha.

The girls lay next to each other on the blanket, staring upwards. The air was chilly, and they snuggled up to each other to stay warm. As their eyes got used to the dark, Emily and Aisha saw the stars glitter like silver pinpricks in a dark blue curtain.

"Wow …" breathed Emily.

"I'm so glad my parents let you stay over," said Aisha happily.

"And not just for one night," said Emily. "A whole week of sleepovers! It's going to be brilliant." She gasped. "Hey, I can see the Big Dipper!" Emily pointed to a small pattern of stars, shaped a bit like a wheelbarrow. "The stars always come out in patterns, called constellations. I've been reading about them. The Big Dipper is part of Ursa Major. Then there's Aquarius, Scorpio ..."

"What about that one?" said Aisha. She pointed to a group of stars that suddenly began to shine brighter than all the others.

Emily frowned. "I don't know ... It's not in my book. It looks almost like ..."

"A unicorn!" said both girls, at the same time.

They sat up and looked at each other, eyes wide. They were thinking of Enchanted Valley, a secret land they had visited together, where unicorns lived with lots of other magical creatures.

Emily reached into her pocket and

drew out the glass unicorn keyring that Aurora, Queen of Enchanted Valley, had given the girls so she could summon them back. To her delight, it was shimmering with multi-coloured lights. "Queen Aurora is calling us again!"

Aisha pulled out her own keyring. It was sparkling too, just like Emily's.

The girls knew what to do. They gently touched the tips of the unicorn horns against each other. At once there was a whooshing sound and a burst of light, like a firework going off. Colourful sparks showered all around. Then the girls felt themselves rising into the air. Their feet left the blanket as they hovered higher.

"We're going back to Enchanted

Valley!" squealed Aisha. She and Emily held hands tightly.

A haze of light glimmered all around. Then slowly they began to drift down, until they landed on a patch of grass.

They weren't in Emily's garden any more. Instead they stood at the bottom of a gentle hill. At the top of it was an elegant golden palace, with turrets shaped like unicorn horns, silhouetted against the purple sky.

"It's twilight in Enchanted Valley, too!" said Aisha. "Wow! Isn't it beautiful?"

"Let's go and see Queen Aurora," said Emily. "I bet she's waiting for us at the palace!"

As the girls climbed the hill, the sky

turned a deeper purple, and shadows crept across the fields and woodland on every side.

Read
# Silvermane Saves the Stars
to find out what adventures are in store for Aisha and Emily!

# Also available

## Book One:

Daisy Meadows

Unicorn Magic

Dawnblaze Saves Summer

From the author of RAINBOW MAGIC

## Book Two:

Daisy Meadows

Unicorn Magic

Shimmerbreeze & the Sky Spell

From the author of RAINBOW MAGIC

## Book Three:

Daisy Meadows

Unicorn Magic

Glitterhoof's Secret Garden

From the author of RAINBOW MAGIC

## Book Four:

Daisy Meadows

Unicorn Magic

Sparklesplash Meets the Mermaids

From the author of RAINBOW MAGIC

# Unicorn Magic

## Look out for the next book!

Daisy Meadows

Unicorn Magic™

Silvermane Saves the Stars

From the author of
RAINBOW MAGIC

If you like
Unicorn Magic,
you'll love...

# Welcome to Animal Ark!

Animal-mad Amelia is sad
about moving house, until she
discovers Animal Ark, where vets look
after all kinds of animals in need.

Join Amelia and her friend Sam for a
brand-new series of animal adventures!